I0527215

Henry E. Turner, Historical Society Rhode Island

## Settlers of Aquidneck

and liberty of conscience. Read before the Rhode Island historical society,

February 1880

Henry E. Turner, Historical Society Rhode Island

**Settlers of Aquidneck**
*and liberty of conscience. Read before the Rhode Island historical society, February 1880*

ISBN/EAN: 9783337378745

Printed in Europe, USA, Canada, Australia, Japan

Cover: Foto ©Andreas Hilbeck / pixelio.de

More available books at **www.hansebooks.com**

# SETTLERS OF AQUIDNECK,

## —AND—

## LIBERTY OF CONSCIENCE,

READ BEFORE THE

## RHODE ISLAND HISTORICAL SOCIETY,

FEBRUARY, 1880.

BY

## HENRY E. TURNER, M. D.

PUBLISHED BY
THE NEWPORT, R. I., HISTORICAL PUBLISHING CO.
R. H. TILLEY, Sec'ry, 128 Thames Street.
1880.

Newport, R. I. :
OLIVER M. ATKINSON, PRINTER.
1880.

# THE AQUIDNECK SETTLERS.

In 1637, what we should call liberal ideas, but what were regarded by the dominant party as heretical delusions, had so far infected the popular mind, in Massachusetts, and especially in Boston, as to have alarmed the authorities and churches in that promising settlement, and caused them serious distrust ; in fact they apprehended that the reign of Belial was at hand, and unless they resorted to stringent measures to rid themselves of the promoters of these errors, they were in immediate danger of being subjected to the dominion of Antichrist.

Accordingly they convened a synod of most of the ministers and many of the prominent laymen of the colony, at Newtown, since Cambridge, (Boston, on account of the poisoned condition of public sentiment, being thought unsuitable,) on the 30th of August, 1637, which remained in session until Sept. 22d, at the close of which the Governor, Mr. Winthrop, proposed that " a like meeting should be held once a year, or at least, the next year, to settle what yet remained to be agreed, or if but to nourish love, &c."

This, however, did not prevail. It might be a curious subject for speculation, how much was left to be disposed of, by an assembly which had been in session 24 days, and had unearthed

and condemned 82 alarming errors prevailing in the community,
and had probably arranged, among themselves, the measures
which should be taken with the recusants.    And also, how the
offending parties appreciated the love, which was proposed to be
cultivated.

At the election, April 17th, 1637, Mr. Vane had been superseded, as Governor, by Mr. Winthrop, and Messrs. Coddington and Dummer by Messrs. Stoughton and Saltonstall, as Assistants, these three were of the heretical faction.

Winthrop says :   [Savage's Winth. Vol. 1, p 219, &c.

" There was great danger of a tumult that day, for those of
that side grew into fierce speeches, and some laid hands on others,
but seeing themselves too weak, they grew quiet."

There is no great matter for wonder in this, for the citizens
of Boston having preferred a petition, and the Governor, Vane,
declining to proceed with the election until the petition had been
read, the other party withdrew from his Presidency, and went
into the election.    This election also was held at Newtown.

[Ibid. Vol. 1, p. 219, & Seq.]

The next day, April 18th, Boston elected as Deputies,
Messrs. Coddington, Vane and Hoffe, (probably Atherton Haugh.)

Winthrop says :   [Ibid. Vol. 1, p. 220 ]

" But the Court being grieved at it, found a means to send
them home again, for that two of the freemen of Boston had not
notice of the election.    So they all went home, and the next
morning they returned the same gentlemen again, upon a new
choice ; and the Court not finding how they might reject them,
they were admitted.

So it appears, they were willing to disfranchise the town of
Boston, but refrained from want of a plausible excuse.

Some recent transactions, in a State not a thousand miles
from Boston, seem to argue, that this enlightened generation
has improved upon this significant example, it is not thought
necessary now to wait for a plausible excuse.

At the Court in the following Nov. a pretext was found, the Deputies from Boston were dismissed or rejected, and Boston, until its principal citizens were banished, was disfranchised.

[Ibid. Vol. 1, p. 245 ]

These Deputies were Coggeshall, Aspinwall and Oliver. The two former of whom were associated in the settlement of Aquidneck, with Coddington, Easton, Clarke, the Hutchinsons and others.

They were all conspicuous adherents of the heretical school, of which the Rev. Mr. Wheelwright was the spiritual leader, and Mrs. Hutchinson the most aggressive propagandist.

The atmosphere of Boston was evidently seriously contaminated by this pestilent heresy, and it became necessary to purge the Colony of Massachusetts Bay, of these heterodox elements.

Accordingly, all the political and hierarchical power of the other towns and churches, was brought into requisition for the accomplishment of that end, and they and their friends were first disarmed, Nov. 27th, 1637, and afterwards kindly permitted to depart the jurisdiction, and humanely relegated to the hospitality and tender mercies of the savage denizens of the wilderness.

Aided by the experience and friendly intervention of Roger Williams, this desperate resource did not fail them, and although the adverse influence of Massachusetts, and of the other neighboring Colonies, forming the league known as the United Colonies of New England, was, for many years, uniformly exercised with the design and purpose to discourage and crush the little community which they established, they, nevertheless, " in the providence of God," with the cooperation of the equally feeble settlements of Providence and Warwick, by conciliatory treatment of the aboriginal inhabitants of the county, and by prudent, industrious and frugal habits, succeeded in establishing the foundation of the little commonwealth, in which we, to-day, so much pride ourselves.

By the friendly and potential intervention of Mr. Williams,

in March, 1637, the Indian chiefs Canonicus and Miantonomi, were induced for a nominal payment of forty fathom of white beads, and gratuity, to the present inhabitants, of ten coats and twenty hoes, (R. I. Col. Rec., Vol. page 46,) to transfer to Wm. Coddington for himself and his associates, the Island of Aquidneck. now Rhode Island, (R. I. Col. Rec , Vol. 1, pp. 50-51,) and in March, 1638, they removed from Massachusetts, and commenced a settlement on the north end of the Island, now Portsmouth, but then known by the name of Pocasset.

This name, in more recent times has been applied to the adjacent territory on the opposite side of the East Bay, now called Tiverton, but evidence is irrefragable, that it was originally applied to the north end of the Island, and to the site of the first English settlement.

An extensive tract of land, in Tiverton, which was then comprised in Plymouth Colonys jurisdiction was granted to 30 persons or shareholders, on the fifth of March, 1679-80, by Plymouth Colony.

The following, which I copy from one of four deeds in first volume Colonial Land Evidence, from Wm. Manchester to different parties, gives the boundary description of the Pocasset purchase, as it was denominated.

" Wm Manchester, of Punkatest, to Matthew Greenell, of Portsmouth, for £13 sterling 1-4 of 1-30 of land at Pocasset, bounded north and west by the Freeman's Lots, next Fall River, west by the Bay or Sound, running between said land and Rhode Island ; south partly by a line that is set at a great rock, on which is a cedar bush, marked near the way that leads into Punkatest; eastward on a pond at Dartmouth town bounds ; westward to Sepowett Creek's mouth, and partly by Dartmouth bounds, and upward into the woods to Middlebury town bounds and Quitquissett Pond, always excepted Suppowett Neck, and the Punkatest meadows, and the land granted Capt. Richard Morris, by Plymouth Court, and that set apart for the ministry."

" All which and some others, I hold under deed of enfeoffment from Plymouth Colony, of date, March 5th, 1679-80."

This deed is dated, Oct. 7, 1681.

He also, Wm. Manchester, sells to John Cooke, Sen., of Portsmouth, 1-2 of 13 shares same purchase, Nov. 24, 1680.

Also, to John Cooke, Sen., 2 shares of same purchase, mentioning as associates in the purchase, Edward Gray, Nathaniel Thomas, Benjamin Church, and others, his friends and partners, Nov. 24, 1680.

The reservations, evidently, were of parcels of land granted by Plymouth, previously to the Pocasset grant.

Whether the name Pocasset was common to Tiverton and Portsmouth, or whether this company of purchasers gave the name to Tiverton, is a question I am not, at present, prepared to discuss.

At a meeting of the body politic, at Newport, Nov 25, 1639, Commissioners were appointed "to negotiate business with our brethren of Pocasset," who could have been no others than the Portsmouth Settlers. [R. I. Col. Rec., Vol. 1, p. 94.]

The name Portsmouth had been adopted July 1, 1639.

[R. I. Col. Rec. Vol. 1, p 72.]

In the description of Wm Coddington's land, as divided in 1640, and which comprises six or seven hundred acres, at and about Coddington's Point, (Pocasset highway forms one of the boundaries,) see First Volume R. I. Rec., Secretary State's Office.

Pocasset therefore, was, without question, the name by which the Indians recognized the north end of Rhode Island.

Shortly before their arrival, viz: March 7th, 1638, the refugees from Massachusetts held a meeting at Providence, and nineteen subscribed their names to the following remarkable covenant, remarkable alike for its sublime simplicity and for the implicit confidence it expresses in the care and guidance of the Divine Spirit.

### THE COMPACT.

"We, whose names are underwritten, do here solemnly, in

the presence of Jehovah, incorporate ourselves into a Body Politick, and as He shall help, will submit our persons, lives and
estates unto our Lord Jesus Christ, the King of Kings and Lord
of Lords, and to all those perfect and most absolute laws of His,
given us in His holy word of truth, to be guided and judged
thereby."

| | |
|---|---|
| Wm. Coddington. | Wm. Dyre. |
| John Clarke. | Wm. Freeborn. |
| Wm. Hutchinson, Jr. | Philip Sherman. |
| John Coggeshall. | John Walker. |
| Wm. Aspinwall. | Richard Carder. |
| Samuel Wilbore. | Wm. Baulston. |
| John Porter. | Edw. Hutchinson, Sen. |
| John Sanford. | Henry Bulle X mark. |
| Edw. Hutchinson, Jr. | Randall Holden. |
| Thomas Savage. | |

To these were added four other names, for some reason,
never, that I am aware, explained, afterwards erased.

At a meeting of the Body, as they expressed it, Aug. 20,
1638, the following were admitted as freemen, with all privileges as themselves, viz :

| | |
|---|---|
| Richard Dummer. | William Brenton. |
| Nicholas Easton. | Robert Harding. |

On the 23d of August, 1638, 13 lots, on the west side of
the Spring, were granted to Mr. Richard Dummer and his
friends, viz :

| | |
|---|---|
| Stephen Dummer. | Mr.          Spencer. |
| Thomas Dummer. | Adam Mott. |
| Mr. (Nicholas) Easton. | Robert Field. |
| Mr. Robert Geoffreys. | James Tarr. |
| Mr. (Osamond) Doutch. | Mr. Robert Harding. |
| William Baker. | |

No do bt Mr. Brenton should have been added to these,
who with Richard Dummer, would make the complement, 13.

At the same meeting it was voted, that Mr. Richard Dummer and his friends should have lands equal to ourselves. Mr. Dummer had been an assistant in Massachusetts, and superseded with Mr. Coddington in the previous year.

Mr. Coddington had been elected Judge; at the first meeting, March 7th, Mr. Aspinwall, Secretary, and Wm. Dyre, Clerk, though why both these offices were thought necessary, does not appear.

The Act constituting the Judge, is as follows:

" We, that are freemen incorporate in this Bodie Politick do elect and constitute William Coddington, Esq, a Judge amongst us, and do covenant to yield all due honour unto him, according to the laws of God, and so far as in us lyes, to maintain the honor and privileges of his place, which shall hereafter be ratified according to God, the Lord helping us so to do."

The obligation taken by Coddington, is:

" I, William Coddington, Esquire, being called and chosen by the Freemen Incorporate of this Bodie Politick, to be a judge amongst them, do covenant to do justice and judgment impartially, according to the laws of God, and to maintain the fundamental rights and privileges of this Bodie Politick, which shall hereafter be ratified, according unto God, the Lord helping us so to do "

(Signed)    William Coddington.

The three clauses constitute their whole Constitution or Organic Law, and the simplicity and directness which characterize it, and the compact and perspicacious manner, in which their subsequent acts are expressed, argues, that if there were any lawyers among them, they must have been of very limited legal accomplishments. They fortunately had very few physicians, and as Edward Johnson says, they were all ministers, they could not be better off in that regard.

January 2d, 1638–9, Mr. Nicholas Easton, Mr. John Coggeshall and Mr. Wm. Brenton were chosen Elders.

At this meeting, the duties of the Judge and Elders are thus defined.

2

" That such, who shall be chosen to the place of Eldership, they are to assist the judges in the execution of justice and judgment, for the regulating and ordering of all offences and offenders ; and for the drawing up and determining of such Rules and Laws, as shall be according to God, which may conduce to the good and welfare of the Commonwealth. And to them is committed, by the Body, the whole care and charge of all the affairs thereof. And that the Judge together with the Elders, shall rule and govern according to the general rule of the word of God ; when they have no particular rule, from God's word, by the Body proscribed, (prescribed) as a direction unto them in the case. And further, it is agreed, and consented unto : That the Judge with the Elders shall be accountable unto the Body, once every quarter of the year, (when as the Body shall be ass mbled) of all such cases, actions and rules, which have passed through their hands, by them to be scanned and weighed by the word of Christ  And if by the Body or any of them, the Lord shall be pleased to dispense light to the contrary of what, by the Judge and Elders, hath been determined formerly, that then and there it shall be repealed as the act of the Body. And if otherwise, that then it shall stand till further light concerning it, for the present to be according to God, and the tender care of indulgent Fathers."

" Given this 2d of 11th, 1638."

At this meeting, the name of Jeremiah Clarke first appears, as a member of the Body, present, when he was admitted does not appear.

Febuary 7th, 1638–9, by Judge and Elders were admitted Freemen :

| Thomas Beeder. | - | Robert Stanton. |
| John Marshall. | | Osamond Doutch. |

Febuary 21st, 1638·9, by Judge and Elders were admitted Freemen :

| Joseph Clarke. | John Driggs. |
| Robert Carr. | |

Up to April 28th. 1639, the original Institution seems to have subsisted, modified by the addition of Elders. Jan. 2d, 1638-9, at that time, a portion of them removed and established themselves at Newport.    Among these were all the prominent officials.

The agreement, under which this settlement was made, was drawn and subscribed before taking their departure from Pocasset, and is as follows :

"Pocasset, on the 28th of the 2d, (month) 1639."

"IT IS AGREED."

" By us, whose names are underwritten, to propagate a Plantation in the midst of the Island or elsewhere.    And do engage ourselves to bear equal charges, answerable to our strength and estates, in common, and that our determination shall be by major voice of Judge and Elders ; the judge to have a double voice."

PRESENT.

| | |
|---|---|
| William Coddington, | Judge. |
| Nicholas Easton, ⎫ | |
| John Coggeshall ⎬ | Elders. |
| William Brentot, ⎭ | |
| John Clarke. | Thomas Hazard. |
| Jeremy Clarke. | Henry Bull. |

William Dyre,    Clerk.

Thirty-two days after, viz. April 30th, 1639, those who remained at Pocasset, entered into the following Compact, viz:

"We whose names are underwritten, do acknowledge ourselves as the legal subjects of (his majestic) King Charles, and in his name, do hereby bind ourselves into a civil Body Politic, unto his laws, according to matters of justice."

| | |
|---|---|
| William Hutchinson. | Anthony Paine. C. Marke. |
| Samuel Hutchinson. | Jobe Hawkins. H. Marke. |
| Samuel Gorton. | Richard Awarde. |
| John Wicks. | John Mow. N. Marke. |
| Richard Maggson. | Nicholas Brown. N. Marke. |
| Thomas Spicer. | Wm. Richardson. X. Marke |

John Roome. R. Marke.

Thomas Beeder H Marke.

Sampson Shotten.

Ralph Earle.

Robert Potter.

Nathanyell Pott·r N Marke.

W. F. Haven. W. T. Marke.

George Chare ꝺ

George Lawton.

John Trippe.

Thomas Layton. T. Marke.

Robert Stanton. S. Marke.

John Briggs. X. Marke.

James Davice. 177 Marke.

John Sloffe. I. Marke.

Erasmus Bullocke.

George Potter. X. Marke.

Four of these are mentioned in Miantonomi's deed of Warwich, besides, Holden, Carder, and Woodel who were residents of Portsmouth, though their names are not attached to this instrument.

Singularly enough, fifteen of these names are signed by mark, though not by any of the Warwick men. On the same date, they elected a judge, supposed to have been Wm. Hutchinson, although, from the defective condition of the records, his name is obliterated. (We depend on Govr. Winthrop's journal for the solution of this problem.)

It appears also, that they elected eight men to assist the Judge, in the duties of administration.

They voted also, that there should be a Court held every Quarter, "to do right between man and man," at which, the Judge and assistants should settle questions not involving an amount exceeding forty shillings, larger amounts requiring a jury of twelve men.

The paucity of records and documents, and the imperfect preservation of those of Portsmouth, (which name the inhabitants of Pocasset adopted, July 1st, 1639,) and the almost total destruction of those of Newport, render the elucidation of the motives which led to this separation, very difficult.

Whether each town had a separate polity, during the year, between March 1639, and March 1640, does not fully appear, but the organization, by Portsmouth, of the full machinery for administration, with a Court of Judicature &c., implies that, for the time being, at least, they recognized no interdependance.

A passage in Govr. Winthrop's Journal, is the only collatteral authority I have been able to find, which alludes to the subject.

(Savages Winthrop, Vol 1. p. 295.)

"Apr. 11, 1639. At Aquiday, the people grew very tumultuous, and put out Mr. Coddington and the other three Magistrates, and chose Mr. Wm. Hutchinson only, a man of a very mild temper and weak parts, and wholly guided by his wife, who had been the beginner of all the former troubles in the country, and still continued to breed disturbance."

In Savage's notes on this passage, Mr. Eddy contradicts this election of Hutchinson in 1639, because the Colonial records do not give it ; but the records of the town of Portsmouth, published many years later than Winthrop's Journal, (1825) confirm Mr Winthrop, as to Mr. Hutchinson's election, or an election, but the rest of the passage must be interpreted in the light of Mr. Winthrop's prejudices and those of his informers, and has no more authority than country gossip ; though he was perfectly sincere in reporting it. It harmonizes too well with his prophetic visions, to provoke any very severe efforts in judical analysis. I may here say, that while Gov. Winthrop's facts are entirely reliable when they occur in his own observation, a great part of them are at second hand, and he cannot be held responsible for them. I say therefore, that Winthrop's Journal although among our best authorities, is not reliable, until carefully and rigidly scaled down.

At the the first organization, March 7, 1638, it is to be observed, Mr. Coddington was elected Judge, but, as far as the records shows, no specifick limitation was assigned for his incumbency; according to modern practice, it would be, by implication, one year: possibly, it was intended to be permanent, according to the official usuages then prevailing in England, or during good behaviour, or during the pleasure of the appointing power. If for one year, then his term would have expired at about the time of removal to Newport.

But, so far as appears by the record no election was held at Newport, in April 1639, either of Judge or Elders. They merely agree to be governed by the major voice of Judge and Elders, in the Plantation which they propose to propagate, and without reference to the settlement or Plantation already made at Pocasset.

The Elders had been elected on the Seventh of November, 1638, their term of service could not then be supposed it expire in April.

The record made in Portsmouth, appears to have been taken to Newport, by the Clerk, Mr. Dyre, who, as well as, the Judge and all three of the Elders, were parties in that settlement, and the records of Newport, to have been kept continuously, in the same book, as the records of Portsmouth were not, and to have been always regarded as an intergral part of the records of the Colony.

It is difficult to understand why, the number of settlers removing, being much the smaller, this should be so, and it is not improbable that there were differences between them, but the records afford no evidence of conflict of authority, and it is certain that after 1648, the time of his suspension, the influence of Coddington was greater in Portsmouth than in Newport. The most probable theory is that the whole Island being common property, the removal to Newport was regarded, as merely a removal of the seat of government, and not necessarily, ever that, for some of the sessions may have been in Portsmouth, and Mr. Brenton was still a resident of Portsmouth, and for several years after, although his name is on the Newport agreement.

It is plain that no grants of land could be secured to grantees, by either town alone.

In the list of those agreeing "to the government of it is or shall be established," Oct. 1st, 1639, are many names of Portsmouth, and many wanting, implying that the necessity for union was felt, generally, but that some of those of Portsmouth, and they the more prominent, were contumacious. This list in-

cluded both towns. None of the Hutchinsons except Samuel,
appear in it, Gorton, Wickes, Shotten and Potter, are on it,
Holden and Carder are not.

Probably, the desire for individual title to the land, was
the most powerful argument for a settlement, as they were issued immediately after its completion, 1641, and none are known
before.

Excepting in relation to negotiations for union, all the
records for this year, indicate legislation for Newport alone.

Unfortunately, the records for this year do not specify the
place where the Court was held, in any case, nor do they give
the names of the persons present, as in other cases.

During this year, 1639-40 not many incidents of great significance, appear upon the records.

May 16. The name of Newport was adopted, applying
to the South and East (and North) from the town to the distance
of five miles, including Middletown, which was set off from
Newport, by the Colonial Legislature, in 1743.

Sept. 2. It was agreed, that the trade "with the Indians
shall be free to all men."

Oct. 8. "It was ordered, that the Judge and Elders shall
meet on the first Tuesday in July, to determine all causes."

At this time, the inconvenience of distinct governments in
so small a territory, seems to have made itself felt, and the following entry was made.

"A catalogue of such (persons) who by general consent of
the Company, were admitted to be inhabitants of the Island
called Aquidneck, having submitted themselves to the government that is or shall be established [therein] according to the
word of God, therein."

Samuel Hutchinson.                              Thomas Emmons.

Richard Award, and fifty-nine others.

This list includes many of both towns, and many are wanting, whence we conclude that there were some, who had not yet
acceeded to the proposed plan of junction, it was nevertheless,

carried into effect, in the March following as we shall see presently.

The record of the same date, has the following entry.

"Inhabitants admitted at the Towne of Nieuport, since the 20th, of the 3d, 1638, forty-two names.

As Newport was not in existence in May 1638, and as scarcely any of these names are on the previous list, I conclude that it has been transposed from some later period, and should have refered to 1639 or 40.

Nov. 28th, 1639. This record appears.

"By the Body Politick in the Isle of Aquethuce Inhabiting this present 25th of 9th month."

In the fourtheenth yeare of the Raign of our Soveraign Lord, King Charles,"

"IT IS AGREED"

"That, as natural subjects of our Prince, and subject to his laws, all matters that concern the peace, shall be, by those that are officers of the peace, transacted, and all actions of the case or debt shall be, in such Courts as, by order, are here and appointed, and by such Judges, as are here deputed, be heard legally determined."

"Given at Nieuport, on the Quarter Court Day, which was adjourned till this day."

"Wm. Dyre, Sec.

On the same date, it was further ordered, that the Commissioners, formerly appointed to negotiate the business with our brethren of Pocasset, shall give them our propositions, under their hands and shall require their propositions, with their answers, and shall give reply unto it, and so, shall return to the Body a Brieve, of what they therein have done.

On the same date, "It was ordered, that Mr. Easson and Mr. John Clarke be desired, to inform Mr. Vane, by writing, of the state of things here, and desire him to treate about the obtaining a Patent of the Island, from his Majestic, and likewise to write to Mr. Thomas Burwood, brother to Mr. Easson, concerning the same thing."

These are all the records of this year, of public interest, and they furnish no hint to any pretension to any jurisdiction, beyond the limts of Newport, nor of any present or past difference with their brethren of Portsmouth, the only intimation of any animosity or difference between them, being the passage in Winthrop's journal, heretofore quoted.

March 12, 1640. A highly important crisis occurred in the fortunes of the infant settlment. A convention of the two towns, was held at Newport.

As far as may be judged from the record, it consisted of eighteen leading citizens of Newport, and ten of Portsmouth, at which, a new form of government, for the whole Island, was established, and officers were elected under it.

Whether the ten Portsmouth men admitted under the third section of the record were present is not made clear, I incline to the opinion that they were, and were part of the convention, in which case, the number from each town would be equal, as follows :

| From Newport. | From Portsmouth. |
|---|---|
| Mr Wm. Coddington, Judge. | Mr. Wm. Hutchinson. |
| " Nicholas Easton, Elder. | " Wm. Balstone. |
| " John Coggeshall, " | " John Sanford. |
| " Wm. Brenton, " | " John Porter. |
| " Robert Jeoffreys, Treas'r. | " Adam Mott. |
| " John Clarke. | " Wm. Freeborne. |
| " Jeremy Clarke. | " John Walker. |
| " Wm. Foster. | " Philip Sherman. |
| " Samuel Wilbore. | " Richard Carder. |
| " Wm. Cowlie. | " Randall Holden. 10. |
| " Thomas Hazard. | " Samuel Hutchinson. |
| " Robert Field. | " Thomas Emons. |
| " Thomas Clarke. | " Job Hawkins. |
| " George Gardner. | " Richard Awards. |
| " Henry Bull. | " Sampson Shotten. |
| " Joseph Clarke. | " Toby Knight, |
| " Robert Stanton | " John Roome. |
| " Wm. Dyre, Secr'y. (18) | " George Barker. (18) |

3

Whether these men were present, as delegates or in their sovereign capacity, does not appear, but, from the purely Democratic forms which they adopted, the latter seems more probable, no record is extant, of the preparatory steps.

The future records of Portsmouth, are all made under the title of Town Meetings, whereas, in 1639, they were recorded as meetings or quarter meetings.

The meetings subsequent to this date, in the General Record, and which, in the printed Record, are under the head of Newport, are always entitled Meetings of the General Court, and were held, interchangably at Newport and Portsmouth.

The record of March 12th, 1640, is as follows :

"At the General Court of Election, held on the twelfth day of the first month, 1640, in the

Towne of Neuport,

present, eighteen as before mentioned.

1.  Mr. William Hutchinson and nine others from Portsmouth, presenting themselves, and desiring to be reunited to this Body, are readily embraced by us."

2.  "It is agreed, by this Body united : that if there shall be anie person found meet for the service of the same, in cyther Plantation, if there be no just exception against him, upon his orderlie presentation, he shall be received as a freeman thereof."

3.  "It is agreed, that Mr. Samuel Hutchinson, (and seven others, of Portsmouth,) are received as Freemen of this Body, fully to enjoy the privileges belonging thereto."

4.  "It is ordered, that the Chiefe Magistrate of this Island, shall be called Governour, and the next, Duputy Governour, and the rest of the Magistrates, Assistants : and this to stand for a Decree."

5.  "It is agreed, that the Governour and two Assistants, shall be chosen from one town, and the Deputy Governour and two Assistants from the other town."

6.  "It is ordered, that the other end of the Island shall be called Portsmouth."

7. The following officers were chosen for one year, or till a new be chosen, viz.:

> Governor, Wm. Coddington, of Newport.
> Deputy Gov'r, Wm. Brenton, of Portsmouth.
> Assistant, Nicholas Easton, of Newport.
> " John Coggeshall, of Newport.
> " Wm. Hutchinson, of Portsmouth.
> " John Porter, of Portsmouth.
> Treasurer, Robert Geoffreys, of Newport.
> " Wm. Balston, of Portsmouth.
> Secretary, Wm. Dyre, of Newport.
> Constable, Jeremy Clarke, of Newport.
> " Mr. Sanford, of Portsmouth.
> Sergeant Attend't, Henry Bull, of Newport.

8 "It is agreed and ordered, that the Governour and Assistants, are invested with the Offices of the Justices of the Peace, according to the Law."

Four other orders of this Court, provide and appoint five from Portsmouth and three from Newport, for the division of lands.

At the General Court, held at Newport, May 6th, 1640, it was ordered,

19. That the particular Courts, consisting of Magistrates and Jurors, shall be holden on the first Tuesday of each month ; and one Court to be held at Nieuport, the other at Portsmouth, and that the sayd Court, shall have full power to judge and determine all such cases and actions, as shall be presented."

"At the General Court, held at
Portsmouth, the 6th of August,
1640,
It was ordered,

23. That each town shall have a joynt and equal supply of the money in the Treasury, for the necessary uses of the same, and that the Governor and one Assistant, from one town, and

the Deputy Governor and one Assistant, from the other town,
shall give a warrant, according to the determination of the major vote of the townsmen, for the same, unto the Treasurer,
which shall be his discharge," and further provides the manner
of keeping his accounts.

25. Provides,

"That each Towne shall have the transaction of the affaires
that shall fall within their own Towne ; and that the Magistrates
of each Towne shall have Libertie to call a Court, every first
Tuesday in the month, at Nuport, and every first Thursday in
the month, at Portsmouth ; wherein actions may be entered, and
juries empannelled, and causes tryed."————"Provided that it
be not in the matter of Life and Limb ; and that if so be a
Plaintiff hath commenced his suit, and the defendant cast, he
shall have libertie to make his appeal to the Quarter Sessions,
which are to be held upon the four Quarter dayes.   And the
two Parliamentarie (or General) Courts to be held on the
Wednesday after the 12th of March, with what time is requisite
thereunto ; and the other the Wednesday after the 12th of Octo-
ber, with what time is requisite thereunto ; which Courts are
equally to be kept at the two Townes.   And what former orders
are repugnant hereunto are hereby nullified."

"For the better understanding of the terme of the four
Quarter dayes, It was, at the next Sessions of the Court General,
determined, that the Quarter Sessions Courts should be held the
Tuesdays (or dayes) before the General Courts ; and the other
two to fall, the one the first Tuesday in July, and the other the
first Tuesday in January."

September 14th.   A session of the General Court was held,
the place not specified ; as the preceding session was at Portsmouth, this was probably at Newport.   At this, nothing trans-
pired of great public significance.

" At the General Court of Election began and held at
Portsmouth, from the 15th of March to the 19th of the same
month.

## 1641.

"The Court roll of Freeman, with the Officers as they were elected, on the 16th of March, 1641."

Mr. Wm. Coddington, Governour, Newport.
"     Wm. Brenton, Dep. Gov., Portsmouth.
"     John Coggeshall, Assis't, Newport
"     Robert Harding, Assis't, Newport.
"     Wm. Balston, Assis't and Treas., Portsmouth.
"     John Porter, Assis't, Portsmouth.
"     Wm. Dyre, Secretary, Newport.
"     Robert Jeoffreys, Treas., Newport.
"     Thos. Gorton, Serg't Attend't, Portsmouth.
"     Henry Bull,      "      "      Newport.
"     Thos. Cornell, Constable, Portsmouth.
"     Henry Bishop,      "      Newport.

And 53 freemen, of whom the last four, Carder, Holden, Shatton and Robert Potter, are in italics, and a note appended, by which they were disfranchised, and their names ordered to be "cancelled out of the roll."

A discussion of this act would not be pertinent to my present purpose; it had no reference to religious faith; they refused to recognize any authority in government, which had no sanction from the Crown, and were, therefore, considered unsafe citizens.

1. "It is ordered and unanimously agreed upon, that the Government which this Bodie Politick doth attend unto, in this Island, is a DEMOCRACIE, or popular Government, that is to say, it is the power of the Body of Freemen orderly assembled, or the major part of them, to make or constitute just Laws, by which they will be regulated, and depute from among themselves such ministers as shall see them faithfully executed between man and man "

4. It is ordered further, by the authority of this present Court, that none be accounted Delinquent for Doctrine: Pro-

vided, it be not repugnant to ye Government and Laws established."

7.    At this session, the dates for Quarter Courts were fixed for the first Tuesdays in March, June, September and December.

12.    The Office of Justice of the Peace was confirmed to the Magistrates.

The Secretary was ordered to transcribe the Laws, and to furnish the town, wherein the Secretary is not a resident, with a copy.

15.    "It is ordered, that a Manual Seale shall be provided for the State, and that the Signett or Emblem thereof shall be a sheafe of arrows bound up, and in the Liess or Bond, this motto indented : '*Amor vincet omnia.*'"

16.    An oath of fidelity was ordered to be taken by the Justices of the Peace, at the Quarter Sessions, of all men or youth above the age of fifteen years.

19.    It is ordered, that the major part of the Courts, being lawfully assembled at the place and hour appointed, shall have full power to transact the business that shall be presented : Provided, it be the major part of the Body entire, if it be the General Court (present,) or the major part of the magistrates, with the Jury in the inferior Courts ; and that such acts concluded and issued, be of as full authority as if they were all present : Provided, there be due and seasonable notice given of every such Court.?'

20.    "It is ordered, established and decreed, unanimouslie, that all men's proprieties in their Lands in the Island, and the jurisdiction thereof, shall be such and so free, that neyther the State, nor any person or persons, shall intrude into it, molest him in itt, to deprive him of anything whatsoever that is or shall be within that or any of the bounds thereof ; and this tenure and propriety of his therein, shall be continued to him or his, or to whomsoever he shall assign it, forever and ever."

The sacred character of the tenure of land, which our forbears entertained, and which the last paragraph so tersely and emphatically expresses, was so thoroughly ingrained in their convictions, that every original grant of land under this dual and yet homogeneous nationality, has, incorporated in it, a copy of this remarkable declaration.

Do I say nationality? It is because they acted under no authority but their own inspired impulse ; they designate their institution the State, and in many instances, "State General," they constitute themselves a Democracy, and establish themselves in a government, in which the officers are elective annually, and whose functions are only ministerial and executive ; and an appeal, in all cases, is reserved to the body of the people, in General Court assembled, which tribunal is to assemble twice in every year, that the streams of justice may not be contaminated by issuing too far from the fountain.

It is true that there were a few faint expressions of loyalty to the Prince, and a few feeble invocations of royal favor and recognition, but surely nothing could be more repugnant to the traditions of the Stuarts, or diverge more widely from the principles of polity which Charles I. and his ministers were disposed to foster.

It is true, also, that Mr. Clarke and Mr. Easton were desired, in view "of the state of things here," to communicate with Mr. Vane, Nov. 30, 1634, and Mr. Burwood, about the obtaining a Patent for the Island, and that Portsmouth, April 30, same year, declared themselves the legal subjects of King Charles, but both these records were made, be it observed, when the two towns were disunited, and felt most sensibly their own weakness.

It is true that, after the Union, the application for a Patent was persisted in, but they probably contemplated nothing more than a confirmation of themselves, in the position they had assumed, of governing themselves in their own manner.

Their applications failed, and when they were authorized

to associate themselves with Providence and Warwick, under the Patent of Providence Plantations, liberal as its provisions were, they were slow to avail themselves of it.

At any rate, from 1640 to 1647, Rhode Island was an autonomous government, as was the State of Rhode Island and Providence Plantations from her declaration of independence, in May, 1776, to the adoption of the Federal Constitution, and during that period Rhode Island was essentially a distinct nationality.

For the years 1645 and 1646, there are no records, and for 1643 and 1644, meagre ones, and probably the previous ones are somewhat defective, but I have endeavored to draw no deductions which are not amply justified by those remaining.

There is no doubt that the book in the secretary's office, from which all these records are derived, is that which is sometimes referred to as the clasped book, and that part of it is lost ; it is certain, at any rate, that many of the deeds made under the division in 1641, are wanting.

### LIBERTY OF CONSCIENCE.

In the original compact, made and subscribed to at Providence, none but divine control is recognized; and submission to the will of the Almighty, according to the laws revealed in his written word, independent of interpretations by creeds or sects, seems to be the chart and compass by which alone they proposed to be guided, on the dark and difficult voyage on which they had embarked ; and surely, although, in some measure, for a certain period, they were compelled to commit themselves to other agencies, they never distrusted the power they had so solemnly invoked, and it were impious to doubt that all other influences were overruled for good, and that, notwithstanding the shortcomings of their progeny, many of the blessings we now enjoy, are the fruits of their humble submission to divine authority, and faith in divine aid and guidance.

At the September session of the General Court, the declaration of March, 1640, was reiterated, in the following terms, to wit :

30. "It is ordered, that the Law of the last Court, made concerning Liberty of Conscience, is perpetuated."

Although, so far as appears, this doctrine was not, until March, 1641, made part of the record, there is no doubt that it was, from the inception of the enterprise, by them, as by the settlers of Providence, recognized as a vital principle in their establishment; in fact, as the corner stone of the structure they proposed to erect.

As appears : This idea was first promulgated at Providence, in a settlement of affairs or covenant, signed by thirty-nine citizens, July 27th, 1640, and it implies that this had always been regarded by them as a principle, if not a recorded obligation.

The clause is as follows, viz. :

"We agree, as formerly hath been the liberties of the town, so still, to hold forth Liberty of Conscience." [Staples' Annals of Providence, page 411 ; and Hazard's State papers, page 465.]

There is also a record of an agreement, signed by thirteen residents of Providence, not including Roger Williams, entering into a town fellowship, and agreeing to be governed "by the major consent of the present inhabitants, masters of families, incorporated together in a town of fellowship, and others whom they shall admit unto them, only in civil things."

This, undoubtedly, was intended to reserve their freedom of belief, though it equally exonerates them from military obligation. This is dated Aug. 20 ; it was probably shortly after their arrival, though the year is not specified.

Joshua Verin's case, for restraining his wife's liberty of conscience, proves the tenacity with which the people of Providence adhered to this provision. [Staples' Annals, Prov. 23-4-5-6 : and Savage's Winthrop, Vol. I, page    ]

On the junction of Newport, Portsmouth, Providence and

4

Warwick, as I shall hereafter show, under the charter of Earl Warwick, the sentiment of the people was most emphatically expressed, in the reaffirmation of this doctrine

All the evidence goes to show that the three settlements of Providence, Warwick and Rhode Island, were entirely in harmony on this point, and equally earnest in making it an integer in their polity.

I take leave to quote from Johnson's "Wonder-working Providence of Sious Saviour, in New England." [Mass. Hist. Soc. Coll. 2d series, Vol. 7, page 24.]

"About this time (1640,) there was a town and church planted at Mount Wollestone, and named Braintree. It was occasioned by some old planters and certain farmers, belonging to the great town of Boston ; they had formerly one Mr. Whelewright to preach unto them, (till this Government could no longer contain them) they, many of them, belonging to the Church of Christ at Boston, but after his departure, they gathered into a Church themselves ; having some enlargement of land, they began to be well peopled, calling to office among them, the reverend and godly Mr. Wm. Thompson and Mr. Henry Flint, the one to the office of a Pastor, the other of a teacher ; the people are purged, by their industry, from the soure leaven of those sinful opinions that began to spread, and if any remain among them, it is very covert, yet the manner of these Erronists that remain in any place, is to countenance all sorts of sinful opinions, as occasions serve, both in Church and Commonwealth, under pretence of Liberty of conscience, (as well their own opinion, as others) by this symbol they may be known in Court and Country."

Johnson, it will be recollected, was one of the Massachusetts commissioners to Warwick in 1643, who exemplified their judicial spirit by marching an army of forty men through Providence, where they had no right, to Warwick, where they had no right, besieging, capturing and taking as prisoners to Boston, all the male population, driving their cattle with them, and leaving the women and children to subsist as they might through the winter, during which time the men were imprisoned in different Massachusetts towns ; the Indians, the while, working their own sweet will with such part of their homes and goods as the marauders did not think it worth their while to carry away.

I never tire of this subject, but my hearers may, but it does not pertain to my subject, and I pass on. I like to quote Johnson ; I have great respect for him ; I believe him entirely sincere in his convictions and entirely truthful as to his facts. He is the incarnation of the repressive spirit which actuated the authorities of Massachusetts, at that time, and for fifty years after, antagonism to which was the appointed mission of Rhode Island.

Other passages from Johnson might be quoted, to prove the abominable and licentious doctrines advocated by Mrs. Hutchinson and her associates, for eighty of which they were arraigned before the Synod of Newton, to twenty-six of which Mrs. Hutchinson plead guilty, but there is abundant justification for the conclusion, that their most flagrant offence, in the eyes of their brethren, was their denial of the coercive power of government over human belief.

And who shall say, that Massachusetts, in all her history for the succeeding fifty years, did not, in her practice, justify her theory ?

Whether they had advanced in their views, may be judged from a quotation from the requisition made on them by King Charles Second's commissioners, Nicoll, Carr, Cartwright and Maverick, May 24th, 1665, proposing certain changes in their laws, adapting them to the Royal Supremacy instead of the Protectoral and Parliamentary, under which they had been framed, a passage in which reads as follows :

"That page 34, heresy and error, ought to be declared with more caution, and a Salvo to the Church of England, and the members thereof."

"That page 36, section 9th, the Law against Quakers, may be restrained, that they may quietly pass about their lawful occasions, though, in other cases, they be punished." [Danforth papers, Mass. Hist. Soc. Coll. Vol. 8, page 86 ]

Previously, May 18, 1665, Col. Richard Nichol, Sir Robert Carr and Mr. Samuel Maverick, had presented themselves to the Court, and Col. Nicoll addressed them. Among other things, he said,

"For the use of the Common Prayer Book. His Majesty doth not impose the use of the Common Prayer Book on any, but he understands that Liberty of Conscience comprehends every man's conscience, as well any particular, and thinks that all his subjects should have, equally, an allowance thereof: he puts no man upon it; but why you should put that restraint on His Majesty's subjects, that live under his obedience, His Majesty doth not understand that you have any such privileges." [Ibid. Vol. 8, page 78-9.]

Also, in a written address, of same date, May 18th, the commissioners say, apparently in answer to a remonstrance from the General Court,

"The end of the first planters coming hither was, as expressed in your address (1660,) the enjoyment of the liberty of your own consciences, which the King is so far from taking away from you, that, by every occasion, he hath promised and assured the full enjoyment of it to you: We therefore admire, that you should deny the Liberty of Conscience to any, especially where the King requires it; and that, upon a vain conceit of your own, that it will disturb your enjoyments, which the King often hath said, it shall not." [Ibid. Vol. 8, page 76.]

His Majesty, in a letter of June 28, 1662, had given them a hint to the same effect. (Ibid. page 52 and seq.)

I here interject, as throwing additional light on the feeling entertained between Rhode Island and the other colonies, on this subject, part of an address to Richard Cromwell, Lord Protector, by the General Assembly of Providence Plantations, May 17, 1659.

"May it please your highness to know, That this poor Colony of Providence Plantations mostly consists of a birth and breeding of the most high, we being an outcast people, formerly from our Mother Nations, in the Bishop's days, and since from the rest of the New English over-zealous Colonies, (bearing with the several judgments of each other, in all the towns of our Colony, the which, our neighbor Colonies do not, which is the only cause of their offence against us,)* our whole frame being much like unto the present frame and constitution of our dearest Mother, England."

This document distinctly verifies the accuracy of the views which the King's Commissioners had imbibed, in relation to Massachusetts at about the same era, or shortly after.

The hints of the Commissioners and of the King, seem to have failed entirely of effect; they were prompted, doubtless, in some degree, by the executions which had occurred not long before.

In 1659, Wm. Robinson and Marmaduke Stevenson; in 1660, Mary Dyer; in 1661, Wm. Leader, had, as the friends' records in Newport say, suffered martyrdom at Boston. And between 1665 and 1675, the notorious persecutions of the founders of the First Baptist Church in Boston occurred, full accounts of which may be found in "Backus' and Benedict's Histories of the Baptists," and in many other authorities, and cover a period of ten years, at least, subsequent to the lectures of the commissioners.

Being traditionally and by conviction, a Congregationalist, I recall, with regret, these phases of puritanical administration, but I should be recreant to my duty, did I overlook them in this case, and while compelled to condemn them, as, in the emphatic expression of the Rhode Island address, "over-zealous," I am proud to say, in the same correspondence with the commissioners, in resisting the threatened usurpations of the Crown, they exhibited a patience, prudence and manly determination. which is worthy of all praise, and which, for a time, averted the humiliation which awaited them in the succeeding reign.

And yet, in the face of the evidence I have thus endeavored to set before you, and various other evidence of the same purport, and in face of the equally well-known and well-established fact, that the governments of Plymouth, New Haven and Connecticut, were in full sympathy with Massachusetts (although their annals are stained by no such acts of outrage,) and that their faces were set, like a flint, against the recusants of Narragansett Bay—at a bi-centennial celebration of the Confederation of the United Colonies of New England, at Boston, in 1843, the spot which reeked with the blood of those martyrs to liberty, John Quincy Adams, than whom, no man on the Continent of America was more familiar with every phase of New England history, who has started on his triumphal march down the ages, as the foremost champion of human liberty in modern times— John Quincy Adams had the hardihood to claim, that to the United Colonies of New England mankind were indebted for the glorious principle of Liberty of Conscience.

And such is history ! "O tempora ! O mores !"

If I were to characterize the histories of New England, as far as I am familiar with them, I should say, that, with a few exceptions, they ought to be collected and published in one set, with uniform binding, and entitled "Bo-ton, a Poem ;" and a very valuable romance it would be. The facts are there, but the analysis, how partial ! the coloring, how fanciful ! The special pleading of the annalists, from whom the data are derived, and who were generally of Massachusetts, and involved in their transactions, has given tone to succeeding histories.

I ask your forbearance while I make a few quotations, proving still further the position of Rhode Island on this question.

"Wm. Arnold to the Governor of Massachusetts," speaking of the Gortonists and Roger Williams, of Providence, says,

"It is a great pity and very unfit, that such a Company as these are, they all stand professed enemies of all the United Colonies, should get a charter for so small a quantity of land, as lyeth in and about Providence, Shawomut, Pawtuxit and Coicit, all which, now Rhode Island is taken out of it.* It is but a small strape of land, lying between the Colonies of Massachusetts, Plymouth and Conitaquot, by which means, if they should get a charter of it, there may come some mischiefe and trouble upon the whole country, if their project be not prevented in time, for under the pretence of Liberty of Conscience, about these partes there comes to live, all the scumme, the runne awayes of the country, which, in tyme, for want of better order, may bring a heavy burthen upon the land.

(Signed) William Arnold.

(dated) Patuxit, this first day of the 7th month, 1651."

[from Hazard's State papers, page 555.]

I find in R. I. State papers, Mass. Hist. Soc. Coll. 2d Series, Vol. 7, p. 79, the following vote of Rhode Island General Assembly, May 19-21, 1647, on organizing under the first charter, at Portsmouth :

"It is agreed by this present Assembly, thus incorporate, and by this present act declared, that the form of government established in Providence Plantations, is Democratical, that is to say, a government held by the free and voluntary consent of all, or the greater part of the free inhabitants.

"And now, to the end that we may give to each other (notwithstanding our different consciences, touching the truth as it is in Jesus,) as good and hopeful assurance as we are able, touching each man's peaceable and quiet enjoyment of his lawful right and liberty. We do agree unto, and, by the authority abovesaid, enact, establish and confirm these orders following."

---

*Referring to Coddington's Perpetual Commission.

This is part of the enacting clause of the code of laws, the concluding paragraph of which code is as follows, and is not in the printed record :

"These are the laws that concern all men, and these are the penalties for the transgressions thereof, which, by common consent, are ratified and established throughout the whole Colony.   And otherwise than thus, what is herein forbidden, all men may walk, as their consciences persuade them, every one in the name of his God.   And let the Lambs of the Most High walk, in this Colony, without molestation, in the name of Jehovah their God, forever."

These papers were furnished, with annotations by Samuel Eddy, Secretary of State, afterwards Chief Justice, and were published in 1826.

Judge Eddy's commentary on this remarkable declaration, is appended, and is as follows :

"The men who, at such a time, and under such circumstances, could frame such a law, and undeviatingly adhere to its principle, though stigmatized as 'heretics, schismatics, antinomians, Anabaptists, Quakers, seekers, soul-murderers, children of Korah, beasts of prey, the very dregs of familism, incendiaries of commonwealths, troublers of churches, and (even in 1809) the rebel band,' or by any or all the opprobrious epithets that bigotry or party zeal can cast upon them, yet, will I reverence, on this side idolatry."

The singular felicity of expression of this note of Judge Eddy's, finds a responsive echo in every true Rhode Island heart, nor can such a limit be put to its magnetic power; it appeals to the æsthetic sensibilities of every individual in all lands, and in all times, whose soul is susceptible to the influences of eternal truth

Our ancestors, therefore, are shown, upon all suitable occasions, to have positively asserted and emphasized their perpetual adhesion to freedom of belief, without qualification, as the sheet anchor on which their institutions depended, and their exact conformity to that principle, in all cases, has never been called in question.

I, as a Rhode Island man, am exceedingly proud of the position assumed and assiduously and pertinaciously adhered to, on the part of the settlers of this colony, and I am, perhaps, unreasonably jealous of any attempt to divide with them the glory, which to them exclusively attaches, of establishing and promoting, for very many years, alone, a government founded upon this essential truth, under every sort of adverse influence ever visited upon men, under like circumstances, and especially do I reprobate and resent a claim of that kind, on behalf of those whose whole influence and effort (and it was exceptionally potential) was strained to its utmost tension to discourage and crush this feeble band, whose only common religion was an adherence to this great vital principle, which was, avowedly, the essential heresy and crime, which, in their eyes justified their consistent and persistent hostility.

How, during the dark and trying period of our eventful history, which closed with the seventeenth century, were the rest of the civilized world engaged? Let the poor, distracted, murdered, pillaged, ravished and tortured Covenanters answer for Scotland. Let the victims of prelatical persecution put in a rejoinder for England. Let the dragonades which watered the fair fields of France with her best blood, tell her story; and the fires, the dungeons, the racks, and all the inconceivable cruelties and atrocities, wring the soul with anguish, for the daily and hourly sufferings of Continental Europe, under the demoniacal inspiration of Torquemada.

We know how it was with the United Colonies While their hearts were agonized by the sufferings of their brethren in England and Scotland, and horrified by the terrible statistics of crime and blood, perpetrated in the name of the gentle Saviour. on the Continent of Europe, they could not grasp the logical

5

sequence of these enormities, they could not yield one jot or
tittle of the right to compel conformity, which, they conceived,
inhered in the anointed of God.

Meanwhile, on this almost infinitesimal point of civilization
and Christianity, and by this little band of obscure individuals,
the spark had been struck, and nursed and fostered in its feeble
glimmerings, and now, behold! in its full blaze it lights all
mankind in the pathway to universal emancipation. What do
not ·Christianity, commerce, science and the arts owe to the
three little communities, which were driven from Massachusetts
for non-conformity to certain tenets, which, if they had any
meaning to the ultra-Puritan mind, are couched in a jargon
which is incomprehensible to the modern understanding!

Our fathers could not have had the remotest conception of the
magnitude and importance of the great work which they inaugu-
rated.   It probably never occurred to them that its benefits ever
would extend beyond their own limits, but they are not the less
entitled to our veneration.   They were the first to plant a community upon the solid foundation of God's everlasting truth,
that no man is answerable for his convictions, except to his
Maker.

All honor to the men who first made it an article of their
constituent law, as all men now acknowledge it to be, of God's
Law.

I would not be understood as disparaging the Puritan
Fathers of Massachusetts, or of Connecticut and Plymouth. God
forbid that any American should withhold his admiration for the
sturdy endurance with which they encountered the political and
religious outrages of the English government and hierarchy, or
the manly heroism with which they braved the perils of the
dreadful ocean voyage, and the still more appalling dangers and
privations of a life in the trackless wilderness, among savages,
in the inhospitable climate, and on the rugged soil of New England, for the sake of an unmolested enjoyment of their religion
and its observances.

They planted, with great care and wisdom, seed which has germinated, and grown, and blossomed, and fructified, and gave a direction to its development, which has made it a nation such as we see ; and who can doubt that the example that they bequeathed, is the great and predominant element to which the success and happiness of this great people is mainly due, and insomuch as we emulate their example, are these blessings likely to be continued to our posterity. Their faults were those of their age, and were few and venial ; their virtues were many and great.

Their failure in tolerance of opinion was universal in that age, and may be palliated on the plea of misplaced zeal, and not judged by the standard of our more enlightened time. In expelling the settlers of this State, "they planted better than they knew."

Providence, Warwick and Rhode Island—we love them all alike ; without all, the settlement would have been a failure. They were one in their devotion to the generic principle, which animated the councils of the Colony, from its inception. The facile tact of Roger Williams paved the way to a friendly relation with the Indians ; the position and character of John Clarke were potential in their negotiations with the Mother Country ; while the nerve and persistency of Holden and Greene assured the retention of Narragansett.

The sheaf of arrows, adopted as an emblem in 1641, would have been peculiarly applicable after the union of all the towns, and the legend, "*Amor vincet omnia,*" was, at all times, appropriate, with those who believed men could be better converted by love than by force ; but the anchor, adopted in 1647, is unexceptionable, expressive of their reliance on a power that can never fail.

Ladies and gentlemen, I thank you for your kind attention, and I ask leave to apologize. First, in that I have had the assurance to come before you for four successive years. I hinted my misgivings (but my friends of the committee overruled my mistrust,) that it would seem to you, as it does to me, like presumption. My excuse must be, my zeal in the cause to which my leisure is devoted.

Second, that I have, as before, given you a large proportion of quotations, probably already familiar, subjecting myself to the criticism of making the text longer than the sermon; but I always feel that a point is better supported by placing the reflections in apposition with the basis on which they are founded.

I trust to your usual indulgent construction.

# APPENDIX.

---

*Remonstrance of Mr. Whelewright's Friends at Court of Election, 1637.*

From Prince Soc. Publications, Hutchinson Papers, Vol. 1, p. 63.

---

"We whose names are underwritten (have diligently observed this honorable Court's proceedings against our dear and reverend brother in Christ, Mr. Wheelwright, now under censure at the Court, for the truth of Christ.) We do humbly beseech this honorable Court to accept this Remonstrance and Petition of ours, in all due submission tendered to your worships.

For first. Whereas our beloved brother, Mr. Wheelwright, is censured for contempt, by the greater part of this honored Court, we desire your worships to consider the sincere intentions of our brother to promote your end in the day of fast, for whereas we do perceive, your principal intention [in the] day of fast, looked chiefly at the public peace of the churches. our reverend brother did, to his best strength, and as the Lord assisted him, labor to promote your end, and therefore endeavored to draw us nearer unto Christ, the head of our union, that so we might be established in peace, which we conceive to be the true way, sanctified of God, to obtain your end, and therefore deserves no such censure, as we conceive.

Secondly. Whereas, our dear brother is censured of sedi-

tion, we beseech your worships to consider that either. the person condemned must be seditious, or must breed sedition in the
hearts of his hearers, or else we know not on what grounds he
shall be censured. Now to the first, we have not heard any
that have witnessed against our brother for any seditious fact.
Secondly, neither was the doctrine itself, being no other but the
very expressions of the Holy Ghost himself, and therefore cannot justly be branded with sedition. Thirdly, if you look at the
effects of his doctrine upon the hearers, it hath not stirred up
sedition in us, not so much as by accident; we have not drawn
the sword, as sometimes Peter did, rashly. neither have we res-
cued our innocent brother, as sometimes the Israelites did Jona-
than, and yet they did not seditiously. The Covenant of free
grace held forth by our brother, hath taught us rather, to become humble suppliants to your worships, and if we could not
prevail. we would rather, with patience, give our cheeks to the
smiters. Since, therefore, the Teacher, the Doctrine, and the
hearers be most free from sedition (as we conceive,) we humbly
beseech you, in the name of the Lord Jesus Christ, your Judge
and ours, and for the honor of this Court, and the proceedings
thereof, that you will be pleased, either to make it appear to us,
and to all the world, to whom the knowledge of all these things
will come, wherein the sedition lies, or else, acquit our brother
of the censure.

Further, we beseech you, remember the old method of Sa-
tan, the ancient enemy of free grace, in all ages of the church,
who hath raised up such calumnies against the faithful Prophet
of God. Eliab was called the troubler of Israel, I. Kings, 18-
17, 18. Amos was charged for conspiracy, Amos, 7-10. Paul
was counted a pestilent fellow, or mover of sedition, and a ring-
leader of a sect, Acts, 24-5. And Christ himself, as well as
Paul, was charged to be a teacher of new doctrine, Mark 1-27;
Acts 17-19. Now we beseech you consider, whether that old
serpent work not, after his old method, even in our days.

Further, we beseech you, consider the danger of meddling against the Prophets, Psalms 105-14, 15 ; for what ye do unto them, the Lord Jesus takes as done unto himself; if you hurt any of his members, the head is very sensible of it ; for so saith the Lord of Hosts. 'He that toucheth you, toucheth the apple of mine eye,' Zach. 2-8. And, 'better a millstone were hanged about our necks, and that we were cast into the sea, than that we should offend any of these little ones which believe on him,' Matthew, 18-6.

And lastly, we beseech you, consider how should you stand, in relation to us, as nursing Fathers, which gives us encouragement, to promote our humble requests to you, or else we would say, with the prophet Isaiah, 22-4. 'Look from me, that I may weep bitterly. Labor not to comfort me,' etc. ; or as Jeremiah, 9-2, 'O, that I had in the wilderness, a lodging place of a wayfaring man.'

And thus have we made known our griefs and desires to your worships, and leave them upon record with the Lord and with you. Knowing that if we should receive repulse from you, with the Lord we shall find grace."

*Commissioners of the United Colonies, N. E.*
*Plym. Col. Records, Vol. IX. Page 151, & seq.*
*Letter from Mass. Sept. 2, 1656.*

———

"HONORED GENTLEMEN—

The remembrance of the solemn covenants and promises
the United Colonies (in the beginning of their combination,)
made one with another, not only to strengthen the hearts and
hands each of others, in the propagating and maintaining of Religion in its purity, but also to be assisting each to other, where
any deficiency, in such respects, may appear ; hath put us upon
the pursuance of our endeavours to discharge our duties, in desiring you to consider of some such meet way and expedient, as
where any defect appears, in any Colony, in the right improve-
ment of such means and ordinances, as the Lord hath appointed
all his to use and improve, for the edification of the body,
whereof Christ is the head, till his second coming.  Having
heard, some time since, that our neighbor's Colony of Plymouth,
our beloved brethren, in a great part seem to be wanting to
themselves, in a due acknowledgment of and encouragement to
the ministers of the Gospel, so as, many pious ministers of the
Gospel have (how justly we know not) deserted their stations,
callings and relations.  Our desire is that some such course
might be taken, as that a pious orthodox ministry might be re-
stated amongst them, that so, the flood of error and principles
of anarchy, which will not long be kept out, where Sathan and
his instruments are so prevalent as to prevail the crying down
of ministry and ministers, may be prevented.

Here have arrived, amongst us, several persons, professing

themselves Quakers, fit instruments to propagate the kingdom of Sathan ; for the securing of ourselves and our neighbors from such pests, we have imprisoned them, till they be despatched away to the place from whence they came, one of which, Richard Smith, we have let out of prison, to return to his family, at Southampton, whence we hope and doubt not, our neighbors of Connecticut will be careful, so to order it, as he may not do the least prejudice, as also, that some general rules may be commended to the several jurisdictions, for the settlement of Government amongst the Indians, that a general law may also be commended to the General Courts, to prohibit the sale of horses to the Indians, or to transport any mares beyond the seas, to Barbadoes or otherwise, on a severe penalty. And that some general rules may be also commended to each General Court, to prevent the coming in amongst us, from foreign places, such notorious heretics as Quakers, Ranters, &c., and that strong waters to the Indians, in all the jurisdictions, may be forbidden, that the name of God be not dishonored.

Naught else, but our best respects to you, and earnest desires that the blessing of the Almighty may be on all your endeavors. Your assured loving friend,

Edward Rawson, Secretary.

Boston, 2 Sept., 1656. By order of the Magistrates."

# ANSWER TO FOREGOING.

*Commissioners U. Colonies to Government of Mass. Sept., 1656. Plym. Col. Records, Vol. I.V. Page 156 and seq.*

———

"The Commissioners, having considered the premises, cannot but acknowledge the godly care and zeal of the gentlemen of the Massachusetts to uphold and maintain those professed ends of coming into these parts, and of the combination of the United Colonies ; which, if not attended in the particulars aforesaid, will be rendered wholly frustrate, the profession miserably scandalized, ourselves become a reproach in the eyes of those that (cannot without admiration) behold our sudden defection from our first principles. We cannot, therefore, but with all earnestness commend it to the wisdom and justice of the several jurisdictions, to take effectual care and make answerable provision, that religion and the ordinances of Christ professed, may be upheld and maintained : which cannot be, but by a due encouragement of an able and orthodox ministry, and a discountenancing of that which is heterodox, and an effectual course to keep out hereticks, the great Engine of Sathan (in these times,) to overthrow the truth ; and because this business is of such high concernment to all, we shall more particularly impart our thoughts to serious consideration.

We cannot, without breach of charity, but take it for a thing granted generally, by the inhabitants of the United Colonies, that an able orthodox ministry is a precious fruit of Christ's death, resurrection and ascension, and necesary for the spiritual good of his people, and to be duly sought after in every society or township within the several jurisdictions.

And secondly, that a competent maintenance proportionable

to the ability of the place, and necessity of the minister, is a debt of justice, and not charity.

Hence thirdly, the minister may justly expect it from the Society and Township wherein he labors.

The reference or relation of a minister being to the whole society jointly, whether in church order or not ; his expectation of maintenance, and the debt of justice, is from the whole society jointly.

Although the society may, according to their own discretion, use divers ways to raise his maintenance, yet, if the ways be ineffectual, though the defect may be by some particular person, yet the Society cannot be discharged, but is the debtor.

The engagement being upon the Society, and that according to right and reason, it necessarily followeth that the Society be enabled with sufficient to itself.

Therefore, the General Courts should declare such a power to be in such Societies, that there may be no pretence in them for want thereof ; and if any Society or Township shall be wanting, either out of neglect or opinion, to procure and maintain, as abovesaid, an orthodox ministry, according to the Gospel, we conceive, by the rules of Scripture and practice, of not only Christian governments, but even of heathen, who not only held their Sacra in veneration, but took care of those that had the keeping of them, and the charge of making known their mysteries.

The several General Courts stand charged with the care that the people professing Christianity own and live according to the rules and ordinances of their profession, and that the dispensers thereof be encouraged as aforesaid ; the maintenance of the ministers being a debt of justice from the Society, and the Society empowered to discharge it ; if any particular person shall be defective to the Society, they ought to be ordered by the ordinary course of justice.

These generals we thought good to propose, from whence

we leave it to the wisdom of the several General Courts, to draw up such conclusions and orders, as may attain the end desired, and if any of the members of the said Courts should not concur (at present) with our apprehensions, we do earnestly desire, that by all means they would labor to inform and satisfy themselves of the truth of the particulars abovesaid, whereof we, for our parts, have no doubt. We do further propose to the several General Courts, that all Quakers, Ranters and other notorious hereticks be prohibited coming into the United Colonies, and if any shall hereafter come or arise amongst us, that they be forthwith secured, or removed out of all the jurisdictions.

That some safe provision be made against selling or giving strong liquors to the Indians, without particular express license from some magistrate, or other officer thereunto deputed, and that upon some weighty occasion or exigent.

And that no horse or mare, young or old, be sold to any Indian, under the penalty of five for one.

And, as to the restraint of sending forth and transporting mares, that each jurisdiction be left at their liberty; and also, that no boats, barques or any tackling belonging thereunto, be sold to any Indian, under the penalty of five for one."

# HERESY AND ERROR.

## Acts of the United Colonies.

## Plym. Col. Records, Vol. I.V. Page 81, Sept., 1646.

---

Upon serious consideration of the spreading nature of error, the dangerous growth and effects thereof in other places, and particularly, how the purity and power, both of religion and of civil order, is already much corrupted, if not wholly lost, in a part of New England, by a licentious liberty granted and settled, whereby many, casting off the rule of the word, profess and practise what is good in their own eyes. And upon information of what petitions have been lately put up in some of the Colonies, against the good and strait ways of Christ, both in the churches and in the Commonwealth, the Commissioners remembering that those Colonies, for themselves and their posterity, did enter into this firm and perpetual league, as for other respects, so, for mutual advice, that the truth and liberties of the Gospel might be preserved and propagated, thought it their duty, seriously to commend it to the care and consideration of each General Court within these United Colonies, that, as they have laid their foundations and measured the temple of God, the worship and worshippers, by that straight reed God hath put into their hands, so they would walk on and build up (all discouragements and difficulties notwithstanding) with an undaunted heart and unwearied hand, according to the same rules and patterns; that a due watch be kept and continued, at the doors of God's house; that none be admitted as members of the body of Christ, but such as hold forth effectual calling, and thereby union, with Christ, the head, and that those whom Christ hath received and enter by an express covenant to attend and observe the laws and duties of that spiritual corporation;

that baptism, the seal of the covenant, be administered only to such members and their immediate seed; that Anabaptism, Familism, Anti-nomianism, and generally all errors of like nature, which oppose, undermine and slight, either the Scriptures, the Sabbath, or other ordinances of God, and bring in and cry up unwarrantable revelations, inventions of men, or any carnal liberty, under a deceitful color of Liberty of Conscience, may be seasonably and duly supprest, though they wish as much forbearance and respect may be had, of tender consciences, seeking light, as may stand with the purity of religion and peace of the Churches. (The Commissioners of Plymouth desire further consideration concerning this advice, given to the General Courts."

*Copy of a Letter from Mr. Roger Williams, President of Providence Plantations, to the General Court of Magistrates and Deputies assembled at Boston.*

*Hutchinson's Original Papers.*
*Hazard's State Papers, Page 610.*

———

"PROVIDENCE, 15, 9 mo., 55 (so-called.

MUCH HONORED SIRS—

It is my humble and earnest petition unto God and you, that you may so be pleased to exercise command over your own spirits, that you may not mind myself nor the English of these parts (unworthy with myself of your eye,) but only that face of equity (English and Christian) which I humbly hope may appear, in these representations following.

First, may it please you to remember, that concerning the town of Warwick (in this Colonie,) there lies a suit of £2,000 damages against you, before his highness and the Lords of his Council, I doubt not, if you so please, but that (as Mr. Winslow and myself had well-nigh ordered it) some gentlemen from yourselves and some from Warwick deputed, may friendly and easily determine that affair between you.

Secondly, the Indians which pretend your name, at Warwick and Pawtuxet, and yet live as barbarously, if not more, than any in the country, please you to know, their insolences upon ourselves and cattel (unto £20 damages per annum,) are insufferable by English spirits; and please you to give credence that to all these, they pretend your name, and affirm that they dare not (for offending you) agree with us, nor come to rules of righteous neighborhood, only they know you favor us not, and therefore send us for redress unto you.

Thirdly, concerning four English families at Pawtuxet, may it please you to remember, that two controversies they have long (under your name) maintained with us, to a constant obstructing of all order and authority amongst us.

To our complaint about our lands, they have lately profest a willingness to arbitrate, but to obey his highness' authority in this Charter, they say they dare not, for your sakes, though they live not by your laws, nor bear your charges nor ours, but evade both, under color of your authoritie."

Honored sirs, I cordially profess it before the most high, that I believe it, if not only they, but ourselves, and all the whole country, by joint consent, were subject to your government, it might be a rich mercy; but as things yet are, and since it pleased, first the Parliament, and then the Lord Admiral and Committee for foreign plantations, and since the Council of State, and lastly the Lord Protector and his Council, to continue us as a distinct Colony, yea, and since it hath pleased yourselves, by public letters, and reference to us from your public Courts, to own the authority of his highness amongst us; be pleased to consider how unsuitable it is for yourselves (if these families of Pawtuxet plead truth,) to be the obstructors of all orderly proceedings amongst us; for I humbly appeal to your own wisdoms and experience, how unlikely it is for a people to be compelled to order and common charges, when others in their bosoms, are by such (seeming) partiality exempted from both.

And therefore (lastly) be pleased to know, that there are (upon the point) but two families which are so obstructive and destructive to an equal proceeding of civil order amongst us; for one of these four families, Stephen Arnold, desires to be uniform with us; a second, Zacharie Rhodes, being in the way of dipping, is (potentially) banished by you. Only Wm. Arnold and Wm. Carpenter (very far also in religion from you, if you knew all.) they have some color, yet in a late conference they all plead that all the obstacle is, their offending of yourselves.

Fourthly, whereas (I humbly conceive,) with the people of this Colony your commerce is as great as with any in the country, and our dangers (being a frontier people to the barbarians) are greater than those of other Colonies, and the ill consequences to yourselves would be not few nor small, and to the whole land, were we first massacred or mastered by them. I pray your æqual and favourable reflection upon that your law, which prohibits us to buy of you all means of our necessary defence of our wives and families (yea in this most bloody and massacring time.)

We are informed that tickets have rarely been denied to any English of the country ; yea, the barbarians (the notorious in lies,) if they profess subjection, they are furnished. Only ourselves, by former and later denial, seem to be devoted to the Indian shambles and massacres.

The barbarians, all the land over, are filled with artillerie and ammunition from the Dutch, openly and horridly, and from all the English over the country (by stealth,) I know they abound so wonderfully, that their activitie and insolencie is grown so high, that they daily consult, and hope, and threaten to render us slaves, as they long since (and now most horribly) have made the Dutch.

For myself (as through God's goodness,) I have refused the gain of thousands by such a murtherous trade, and think no law yet extant amongst yourselves or us, secure enough against such a villanie ; so I am loath to see so many hundreds (if not some thousands,) in this Colonie, destroyed like fools and beasts, without resistance. I grieve that so much blood should cry against yourselves ; yea, and I grieve that (at this instant, by these ships) this cry and the premises should now trouble his highness and his Council. For the seasonable preventing of which, is this humble address presented to your wisdom, by him who desires to be,

Your unfeigned and faithful servant,

Roger Williams,

of Providence Plantations,

President."

[*Postcript to Above Letter.*]

"Hon. Sirs:

Since my Letter, it comes into my heart to pray your leave to add a word as to myself, viz.: At my last return from England, I presented your then honored Governor, Mr. Bellingham, with an order of the Lords of the Council, for my free taking ship or landing at your parts, unto which it pleased Mr. Bellingham to send me his assent in writing. I humbly crave the recording of it by yourselves, lest forgetfulness hereafter again put me upon such distresses as, God knows, I suffered when I last past through your Colony to our native country.

R. W."

*Copy of a Letter fro.n Providence Plantations, to the General Court of the Massachusells.*

*Hutchinson's Original Papers.*

*Hazard's State Papers, Page 612.*

———

"PROVIDENCE, 12, 3 mo., 56 (so-called.

May it please this much honored Assembly to remember that, as an officer and in the name of Providence Colonie, I presented you with our humble requests, before winter, unto which, not receiving answer. I addressed myself, this spring, to your much-honored Governor, who was pleased to advise our sending of some of Providence to your Assembly.

Honored sirs, our first request (in short) was and is, for your favorable consideration of the long and lamentable condition of the town of Warwick, which hath been thus. They are so dangerously and so vexatiously intermingled with the Barbarians, that I have long admired the wonderful power of God in restraining and preventing very great fires of mutual slaughters breaking forth between them.

Your wisdoms know the inhumane insultations of these wild creatures, and you may be pleased to imagine, that they have not been sparing of your name, as the patron of all their wickedness against our English men, women and children, and cattle, to the yearly damage of 60, 80 and £100

The remedie is (under God,) only your pleasure that Pumham shall come to an agreement with the town or Colonie, and that some convenient way or time be set for their removal.

And that your wisdoms may see just grounds for such your willingness, be pleased to be informed of a realitie of a solemn covenant between this town of Warwick and Pumham, unto which, notwithstanding that he pleads being drawn to it by the awe of his superior Sachims, yet I humbly offer that what was done, was according to the law and tenor of the natives (I take it) in all New England and America, viz.: that the inferior Sachims and subjects shall plant and remove at the pleasure of the highest and supreme Sachims, and I humbly conceive that it pleaseth the most high and only wise to make use of such a bond of authoritie over them, without which they could not long subsist in humane societies, in this wild condition, wherein they are.

2.    Please you not to be insensible of the slipperie and dangerous condition of this, their intermingled cohabitation.    I am humbly confident, that all the English towns and plantations in all New England put together, suffer not such molestation from the natives as this one town and people.   It is so great and so oppressive that I have daily feared the tidings of some public fire and mischief.

3.    Be pleased to review this copie from the Lord Admiral, and that this English town of Warwick should proceed, also, that if any of yours were there planted, they should, by your authoritie, be removed.   And we humbly conceive, that if the English (whose removes are difficult and chargeable,) how much more these wild ones, who remove with little more trouble and damage than the wild beasts of the wilderness.

4.    Please you to be informed, that this small neck (wherein they keep and mingle fields with the English) is a very den of wickedness, where they not only practice the horrid barbarisms of all kinds of whoredoms, idolotries and conjurations, but, living without all exercise of actual authoritie, and getting store of liquors (to our grief,) there is a confluence and rendezvous of all the wildest and most licentious natives and practices of the whole country.

5.    Beside satisfaction to Pumham and the former inhabitants

of this neck, there is a competitor who must also be satisfied, another sachim, one Nawwashawsuck, who (living with Ousam-aquin) lays claim to this place, and are at daily feud with Pum-ham (to my knowledge,) about the title and lordship of it. Hos-tilitie is daily threatened.

Our second request concerns two or three English families at Pawtuxet, who, before our charter, subjected themselves unto your jurisdiction. It is true, there are many grievances between many of the town of Providence and them, and these, I humbly conceive, may best be ordered to be composed by reference.

2. But we have formerly made our addresses, and now do, for your prudent removal of this great and long obstruction to all due order and regular proceedings among us, viz.: the refusal of these families (pretending your name) to conform with us, unto his highness' authoritie among us.

3. Your wisdoms experimentally know how apt men are to stumble at such an exemption from all duties and services, from all rates and charges, either with yourselves or us.

4. This obstruction is so great and constant, that (without your prudent removal of it) it is impossible that either his High-ness or yourselves can expect such satisfaction and observance from us, as we desire to render.

Lastly, as before, we promised satisfaction to the natives at Warwick (and shall, all possible ways, endeavor their content,) so we humbly offer, as to these, our countrymen, First, as to grievances depending, that references may settle them. Sec-ondly, for the future, the way will be open for their enjoyment of votes and privileges, of choosing and being chosen to any of-fice in town or colonie.

Our third request is, for your favorable leave to us to buy of your merchants, four or more barrells of powder, yearly, with some convenient portion of artillerie, considering our hazardous frontier situation to these Barbarians, who, from their abundant supply of arms, from the Dutch (and perfidious English, all the land over,) are full of our artillerie, which hath rendered them exceedingly insolent, provoking and threatening, especially the inlanders, which have their supply from the fort of Aurania. We have been esteemed, by some of you, as your thornie hedge, on this side of you; if so, yet an hedge to be maintained; if as out sentinels, yet not to be discouraged. And if there be a jealousy of the ill-use of such a favor, please you to be assured, that a credible person in each town shall have the dispose and managing of such supplies, according to the true intent and purpose.

For the obtaining of these, our just and necessary petitions, we have no inducement or hope from ourselves. Only we pray you to remember, that the matters prayed, are no way dishonorable to yourselves, and we humbly conceive do greatly promote the honor and pleasure of his Highness, yea, of the Most High also, and lastly, such kindnesses will be obligations on us, to studie to declare ourselves, upon all occasions,

Your most humble and faithful servants,

Roger Williams, President.

In the name and by the appointment of

Providence Colony.

P. S. Honored gentlemen, I pray your patience to one word, relating to myself only. Whereas, upon an order from the Lords of his Highness' Council, for my future security in taking ships and landing in your ports, it pleased your honored then Governor, Mr. Bellingham, to obey that order, under his own hand, I now pray the confirmation of it, from one word of this honored Court assembled.        R. W."

*Copy of a Letter from Mr. Roger Williams to the General Court.*

*Hutchinson's Original Papers.*

*Hazard's State Papers, Page 615.*

———

"Boston, 17, 3, 56, (so called.)

May it please this much honored Assembly,

I do humbly hope that your own breasts and the publick shall reap the fruit of your gentleness and patience in these barbarous transactions, and I do cordially promise for myself (and all I can perswade with,) to study gratitude and faythfulness to your service.

I have debated with Pumham (and some of the natives helping with me,) who shewed him the vexatious life he lives in, your great respect and care toward him, by which he may abundantly mend himself, and be united in some convenience unto their neighborhood and your service. But I humbly conceive, in his case, that *"dies et quies sanant hominem,"* and he must have some longer breathing, for he tells me that the appearance of this competitor, Nawwushawsuck, had stab'd him. May you, therefore, please to grant him and me some longer time of conference, either until your next general assembling, or longer, at your pleasures.

My other requests, I shall not be importune to press on your great affairs, but shall make my address unto your Secretarie, to receive by him your pleasure.

Honored gentlemen,

Your humble and thankful servant,

R. W."